Insects Use Color

Written by Dr. Simon Pollard

Insects can use color to tell other animals to stay away. They use color to help them look like other insects. They can use color to trick other animals, too.

This butterfly has lots of colors,
and it is easy to see.
Some animals like to eat butterflies,
but they will not eat this butterfly.
The colors tell other animals
that this butterfly tastes bad.

monarch butterfly

This butterfly is easy to see, too.
But it can trick other animals!
It can copy the colors
of butterflies that taste bad.
Then it won't be eaten.

viceroy butterfly

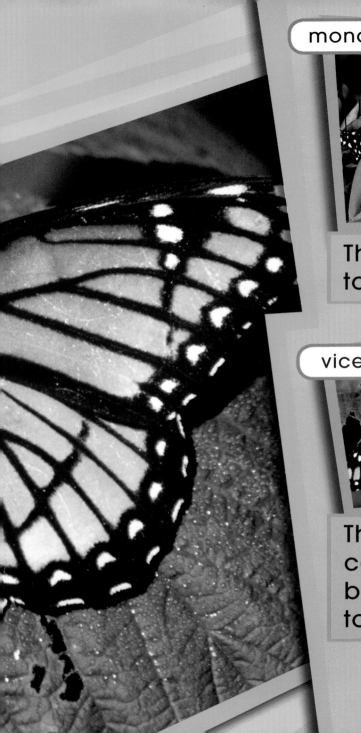

monarch butterfly

This butterfly tastes bad.

viceroy butterfly

This butterfly copies the butterfly that tastes bad.

7

Some insects use color
to make them look bigger!
Butterflies and moths can have
big colored spots on their wings.
The spots are called eyespots.
They can trick other animals.

moth

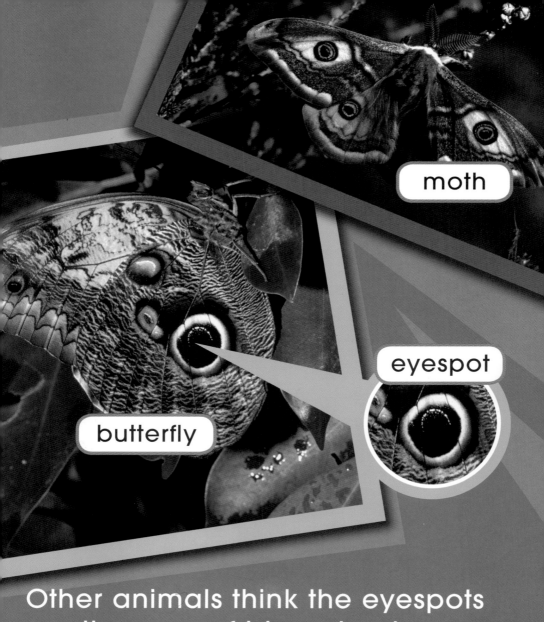

moth

eyespot

butterfly

Other animals think the eyespots
are the eyes of big animals.
They will stay away.

9

Some caterpillars use color
and eyespots to keep safe, too.
Look at the eyespots
on this caterpillar's head.
The eyespots make it look
like an animal with big eyes.

eyespot

eyespot

This caterpillar is very clever.
It can trick other animals, too.
The caterpillar can hang
upside down and flash its eyespots.
The eyespots make it
look like a snake.
It is the color of a snake, too!
Other animals will know
to stay away.

eyespot

Insects can use color in different ways to keep them safe.

moth

wasp

Index

▬▬▬ **Guide Notes**

Title: Insects That Use Color
Stage: Early (4) – Green

Genre: Nonfiction
Approach: Guided Reading
Processes: Thinking Critically, Exploring Language, Processing Information
Written and Visual Focus: Photographs (static images), Index, Labels, Captions, Comparison Diagram
Word Count: 222

THINKING CRITICALLY
(sample questions)

- Look at the front cover and the title. Ask the children what they know about insects that use color.
- Look at the title and read it to the children.
- Focus the children's attention on the index. Ask: "What are you going to find out about in this book?"
- If you want to find out about a caterpillar that can trick other animals, what pages would you look on?
- If you want to find out about a butterfly that tastes bad, what page would you look on?
- Look at pages 6 and 7. How do you think the butterfly can copy the colors of other animals?
- Look at pages 12 and 13. Why do you think other animals will stay away from the caterpillar if it looks like a snake?

EXPLORING LANGUAGE

Terminology
Title, cover, photographs, author, photographers

Vocabulary
Interest words: butterfly, insects, moths, caterpillar, snake, eyespots
High-frequency words: know, head
Positional words: on, upside down, in
Compound words: butterflies, eyespots, upside

Print Conventions
Capital letter for sentence beginnings, periods, commas, exclamation marks, possessive apostrophe